PATCHWORK

GOES UNDER COVER

Patchwork Goes Under Cover

Illustrations © 2014 Jacqueline Schmidt
Text © Benjamin Mott

Published by POW!
a division of PowerHouse Packaging & Supply, Inc.

Library of Congress Control Number: 2014937067

37 Main Street, Brooklyn, NY 11201-1021
info@POWKidsbooks.com
www.POWKidsbooks.com
www.PowerHousebooks.com
www.PowerHousePackaging.com

ISBN: 978-1-57687-717-3

Art direction by Krzysztof Poluchowicz

10 9 8 7 6 5 4 3 2 1

Printed in Malaysia

PATCHWORK

GOES UNDER COVER

JACQUELINE SCHMIDT

Brooklyn, NY

Patchwork's a hodgepidge,
Part stuffing, Part bear;

When it's cold outside,
he wears a snowsuit made of hair.

When wintertime comes,
his Bear friends must snooze.

But a cave won't suit Patchwork,
so he heads out for a cruise.

"We huddle together,
and stay on our feet!"

"Hey, Whale!" says Patchwork, "When do you sleep?"
"I snooze while I swim, but never down deep."

"Hello, Honey Bees!
Do you ever catch some ZZZs?"

"When we're too sleepy to flap, we just take a nap."

"Do Butterflies doze,
what are the chances?"

"Yes, we hang upside down
beneath leaves and branches."

"Hedgehog, Possum, and Owls,
did you stay up all night?"

Woodchuck says, "Yes, but they sleep
through the day, so nighttime's all right."

"Dear Crows,
are you weary from flapping and flying?"

"We sleep in the trees
while the wind is gently sighing."

"Farm friends keep busy,
there's so much to do."

Patchwork said to himself,
"Since we all need to rest,

So off to Patchwork's house
the menagerie went:

Giraffe, Zebra, Birds, and a small Fox from Kent.

Here's a morsel of cheese,
and a strawberry, too."

They Played on Pillow Mountain, laughing and leaping,
Until even the Bears thought about sleeping.

They all brushed their teeth and got ready for bed.
And everyone agreed that a book should be read.

Then they all slept, and dreamed through the night,

Of Dinosaurs, and Planets,
and Bears in flight